DREAMS

by Peter Spier

Doubleday & Company, Inc., Garden City, New York

Library of Congress Catalog Card Number 85-13130   ISBN: 0-385-19336-X Trade

0-385-19337-8 Prebound   Text and illustrations copyright © 1986 by Peter Spier   All rights reserved

Printed in the United States of America   First Edition

...and the next time you gaze at the sky: dream dreams!